T0147729

"Nwilo is a vibrant new voice in Nigerian literature. Listen to him."

E.C. Osondu – Winner, The Caine Prize for Africa

Nwilo's writing captures the joy, hope and pain of Africa.

Elaine Pillay – (South Africa)

Nwilo writes with a quiet and fiery validation of African Englishes, specifically a certain Nigerian English - how refreshing! This is exactly the sort of re-imaginative work that lovers of African fiction have been awaiting. A Tiny Place Called Happiness is a triumph for orature in literature everywhere!

Donald Molosi, Author, *We Are All Blue.*

This short story collection understands the narrative of the voiceless. It brings together the lives of dreamers and dreams from the Niger-Delta area of Nigeria—mostly, using experimental and diverse style to explore the human condition. The stories in the collection bring us to a homeland we do not see, and the writer, in turn, offers the narrated tough circumstances of his characters in tender words. Nwilo writes like an aspiration--his voice desires to try many things and this is the reason we should heed this writer with many stories to tell.

Jumoke Verissimo – Author, *I am Memory, The Birth of Illusion*

A TINY
PLACE CALLED
HAPPINESS

STORIES

BURA-BARI NWILO

Baron Cafe

Published in Nigeria in 2016 by
Barons Cafe

An imprint of Fairchild Media
Plot 1-4 Adewumi Layout, Akinyemi, Ibadan, Nigeria
+2348181880536 | +2348068108018
Email: cafe@fairchildng.com

ISBN: 978-978-52838-2-2

Cover Design: Prince Smart
Photography: TJ Dan (Photo of Bura-Bari Nwilo)
Design and Layout: Babajide A. Alabi

Dedication

To my inadequacies

Happiness is not one thing.

It could be anything.

It could be nothing.

PORT HARCOURT

PORT HARCOURT

It was not past midnight. Maybe it was but there was nothing indicative of the time, for moonlight lit the country. Men and women lined up the street, seated behind coolers on makeshift tables, selling alcohol, condoms and information to customers, according to needs. Behind the women, taxi drivers sat on the bonnet of their cars and cracked jokes whenever a drunken man or woman laughed out of Eddy's bar, holding a partner. And when a customer showed up, they rushed at him or cursed below their breath when he complained of prices. But Fole and Hennel did not care much for the onlookers who whispered what a lucky woman Fole was to have caught a whitie, a rare sight at the bar.

Solar powered streetlights enhanced the light from the moon and one could take a photo on the street without additional light. Beneath the streetlights, their reflections cuddled tighter than they did in reality, like they were made into each other, like a pair of trousers, clean, perfumed and perfected. A good dance was what they wanted and a brief one at the bar was enough for the day. The Nigerian songs had Hennel dance like an overfed frog, bending low and twisting in same way to all songs played. And while the songs played on endlessly and his glass of whiskey was refilled, he spent more time behind Fole, rocking and rubbing his groin against her. Or maybe that was it, a spice to the dance.

Hennel wrapped his arms around the waist of the less taller Fole so that she walked like she was injured around the ribs. And Hennel's kisses on her nose drew out sharp laughter from her that fell in between their conversation. Time had not been exactly fast for Fole. It had nothing to do with anything, really. Maybe a hand held it still or maybe it had something to do with how the week was spent; from a masquerade entertainment to swimming at the hotel where Hennel stayed. And of course, the poetry-reading they attended, where Hennel read her a poem by Walt Whitman.

Hennel who had visited from Harvard had only placed a call three days earlier to know if Fole was doing well. He had not told her he would visit Port Harcourt soon. She knew he would visit Nigeria later in the year but was not particularly sure when it would be. Her MFA degree rested the moment she got to Nigeria from Boston. Her dad spoke to someone who knew someone powerful and she got a job at a Mobil zonal office. With great salary and amazing benefit, she knew writing had to take a fine seat at the rear while she took care of responsibilities like the first daughter she was.

"I thought your visit would be during summer, Henz?"

"This, here with you, is summer, Fole."

She had suggested that he should come to Port Harcourt to see her but that was a romance-induced thought, such that you say before you kiss your lover over the telephone and end the call and blush. Hennel's interest came almost at the end of their writing programme. She had given up the hope of a relationship when it happened.

When Hennel landed at the Port Harcourt airport, he hired an eloquent airport taxi driver who he paid to speak politely and polished to Fole, to say he was bringing items someone close to her had sent through. She gave out her office address and when the door slid open, it was Hennel, same bald, gap toothed and skinny clown who had made her consider taking a trip to Switzerland, smiling at her with spread arms. For a moment, Fole thought it was unreal, his surprise visit. And he had changed a little since their MFA. But this, the surprise visit was just too much for a lone girl who had stayed a bit mindful of men for two years, not that she did

11

not meet bald men who found her attractive but conversation always went awry. What she got were very pale talks; politics, about a changed government that was going to improve electricity, or those who shared images of how they were customers of the big stores in Dubai where they would take her shopping. She, a bit old-schooled, wanted the talks of flowers, of how they were in varieties and some with high sensitivity that if you spoke harshly around them they could hear you and recoil. She wanted the story of bleeding grasses, how they cried and produced special scents because they were dying — mundane things, like the men called it. And Fole wanted some gossip, of the latest fight in the literary circle, of how someone has written of V.S. Naipaul in The New Yorker as so old he could not recognise his own books at book festivals.

Hennel had his moment at being boring and insensitive; when his stories would not come and when he probably could not find a certain anthology of stories needed to spark off his muse. But standing before her was Hennel, the first man who didn't start a conversation with greetings, like she was some royalty. He had brought his tray of food to her table and had nosily chewed on his food until Fole quietly left the table for another one, hoping his demon would die down but Hennel, an un-royal pain in the butt, went after her and asked if she was offended and said he would kiss her if she wasn't and the laughter that followed became the friendship that spanned two years.

The couple slowed their pace and held hands.

"I'm afraid I'd miss you terribly," Hennel muttered through a kiss.

"You could stay a little longer," Fole said, avoiding his eyes.

"And what would I be doing in Port Harcourt?"

"Staying with me," Fole threw him a love-punch.

"That's not a job, Fole."

"It is, now."

They giggled. A man, who had followed them, one of those who whispered when they stepped out of the bar, met them with a leather strap-bag. He said it was theirs, that they had dropped it while dancing at the bar. But the confusion on the faces of the couple didn't settle when a shiny metal emerged from the bag and pointed at them. Frozen, Fole's shoes, her favourite heels, and Hennel's Hublot wristwatch went with the borrower, a term Fole later learned. To her, borrower made more sense than the word thief, for all that was taken from someone forcefully was returned by the universe in the most unexpected way.

And the next morning, Fole did not insist that Hennel stayed. She kissed him and said they'd meet again, someday, in the US, Switzerland or Paris, or wherever it was that awaited them.

THE SILLY BUT FABULOUS LIFE OF VINCENT PIGIRI

THE SILLY BUT FABULOUS LIFE OF VINCENT PIGIRI

Vince finished his university degree six years before we began dreaming about JAMB and how a university campus looked like. He was the big brother on the street that everyone wanted to become, for he read books always, until his stay at home became such a plague that parents pointed at him when they were angry, as a bad example, a person no child should emulate. Even if the government didn't provide any job, how difficult was it for Vincent to create a small job for himself, the people on the street gossiped. He could be like other graduates who finished same time as him but did not just sit at a spot with a book; they sneered and made faces when he walked.

When Vincent's luck glowed, everyone affirmed that something was not right for it was fabulous. But who openly spoke against the beautification of someone who had been ugly all his life if not a demon, an enemy of progress?

At the initial stage of his glory, Vince smiled more and barely accepted money from his friends when they came by in their cars. He looked at them and smiled and looked at their cars; its stretch and freshness, and smiled even broader but no one knew what it was that went up in his mind. Sometimes the people whispered that he was going mad despite changed clothes and a shaved face. Other times, when he stopped the weird smile and asked where his friends had bought their cars, they drove off, summarising his question as evidence of a lost mind.

As Vincent's grace increased, his shoes and clothes changed, and his breath had mint in it. When he walked up to a woman and asked for her name and phone number, he got them with ease. His beards were finely trimmed and carved, showing off his goatee, which gave him the look of someone whose miracle had arrived in a ship. If a child was crying on his way to anywhere, Vincent stopped, carried the baby and rocked him until he would smile. If an older woman was struggling to lift a gallon of water to her head, he walked up to her and kindly asked where her house was, and in all cheerfulness, he would carry the gallon of water towards the location.

Gradually, everyone liked Vincent again but in a very suspicious way, like he was a time bomb everyone feared would explode someday.

When Vince gambled, his numbers were the lucky ones. When someone's car broke down and they struggled with it, putting water where it should be and fuel where it was supposed to go, and the vehicle did not pick up, Vincent fixed it. Then one day, someone quite observant but driven by sheer jealousy whispered to another person who shared the gossip with another person, that Vincent had a water-wife with whom he had mated and whose powers were active in his life. And maybe it was true, because Vincent didn't call the phone numbers he got from the women he met, neither did he bother to take them out or discus his bed and his manliness with them. He looked happier, unconcerned with frivolities and dressed in finer clothes daily. And it was also rumoured on the street that Vincent was preparing to buy a car, not a used vehicle from someone in Europe who was tired of the machine but a brand new beast that no one had driven.

And so it became a norm in the community that the people who went to church used Vincent's situation as prayer-points. They asked that the God who turned around Vincent's situation after six years of joblessness and misery, of living on friends and talking to himself, they asked that same God should answer them and make all things anew. And maybe

God didn't hear them or that he was probably busy with other things, like assisting Vincent build a fine bungalow in the community, one whose marble he was importing from Italy. And the pool, a mason had told someone, was the finest thing he had ever seen. The sets of furniture too were sensitive. When one wanted to sit down, he snapped fingers and the chairs rolled out finely and when one was done, they rolled away quietly. The security light outside his gate woke up each time someone passed his compound.

Vincent Pigiri gradually befriended the local church priest and the friendship caught fire quickly because each visit he made brought wads of notes and bags of rice. So when a list of a younger batch of knights was drafted, Vincent's name sat on the very top. He was on his way of becoming a mayor too for he was a graduate and a businessman who was not coming into politics to feed on the peoples' wealth but to pump in his own contributions. And maybe fix the streets of Bori so the roads could be constructed without project funds missing, and there would be electricity so smaller businesses could thrive. But as things grew finely for Vincent so was his pact with Satan, or God. One day, an observant and jealous man in his community, keeping watch at night, saw a drop-off, a headless body of a child thrown to the roadside. He fired a shot at the person who had dumped the body and the figure which grumbled in pains of gunshot and fell to his knees was not of a stranger but of Vincent, a knight-to-be and the mayoral candidate of Bori.

LIKE EYES LIQUID WITH HOPE

LIKE EYES LIQUID WITH HOPE

TODAY, I AM Oga, the alternate Oga of the house. It is a very good thing. I can go to the Big Oga's wardrobe and pick any of his big, nice smelling clothes and wear. I may wobble in his coat but that would only be until I start drinking beer. But some words sef has issues. 'Wobbling!' It is a bad word meant for small people like me who have very small flesh. People like Oga who talk too much grammar must have invented it to suppress us. It does not have anything to do with him and his size. Wobbling! It is me. The word has me as its profile picture. Which kain yeye thing is that?

Anyway, I don't have to worry my head about the trouble that won't finish. English is madness. Who does not know it? Was it not the fear of English that drove the baboon into the forest? If I fight this big word today won't the people who own the world invent another bigger one? People are heartless. They have taken their hearts into their palms and rubbed it with so much nonsense. Nothing in this world moves them. They could bring one that would break my jaw and render me totally useless. Will I keep fighting big big words until the world finishes? Who has that kind of power? Do I look like Jesus Christ that will go and carry the wahala of people on his head, and follow them and go and die on a cross? Am I foolish? Was I born today? Had Cecilia Deemua, my wonderful mother given birth to a national mumu? Hian. This thing is really causing me to fear oh. But as for my Oga, I can touch his shoes or even try it on. I can walk about and make the noise that won't pass through the big door or that nonsense gateman would run his stupid mouth and spoil my Egusi soup with his yeye Okra soup.

It is a good thing to be the alternate Oga. But Nneka won't respect me. That girl has problem with her head. Her office in the kitchen has made her begin to think that she is equal with me in rank. She is too strong inside her head. If you talk one she will talk one hundred. Yes. One hundred words in one small minute. Who does that kind of thing? Her mouth runs like borehole. She would say: see this yeye Ogoni boy oh. Na you I come city come work for? You don't know that I am getting married soon to a rich man and I will be in my husband's house, commanding house-boys like you wey no get fear for eye? You hear? She is like that. She no get even small respect, like small one that can fit inside tin-tomato container. I mean the small tin-tomato oh. She dey behave like say dem no use hot water press sense into her head when she was born. If I call her and say: Nne, come! Bring me garri and soup with roasted meat. She fit even slap me sef. She go come and stand for my front, shake her yansh and tell me to go jump inside lagoon and die. You see, see women of these days? Dem no get fear of God inside their body. In short, God has died and been buried inside their heart.

If I was her I would treat me like an alternate Oga whose situation can change tomorrow. Situation changes oh. I have seen a man who started as a boy in his Oga's house. Today, when he drives, his Oga will carry computer and look the type of car that his boy is now driving. He is proud of the boy. He goes to everywhere with high shoulder, preaching what a better Oga he was to Rufus. Yeye dey smell. But Nneka won't even treat me like the temporal Oga with potential. No. Sense no dey inside her dictionary. In fact, if you carry two hands open inside her dictionary, na either carrot, green pepper, yellow tomatoes, or vegetable na you go see. Nothing wey get value settle inside that her head. Imagine sey she humble herself, serve me food, won't I sit and enjoy mysef and add two minutes fat to my bones? If she did I would have myself all the food in the house and chop until I am tired. I would sit and she would bring me water to wash my hands, kneeling down, of course. But whether she likes it or not, I am the alternate Oga and with or without food, no one will spoil my groove. I will not allow that arrant nonsense in this house. Na rat get house when Oga comot. Today na my own Christmas and anybody wey come become witch I will use prayer and fasting kill am. Oga told madam that when Small Madam will come back that he will use Holy Water wey him bishop give am take bath small madam. But that one brought laughter. Madam laugh sotey she almost fall for ground. I did not know that there was so much laughter inside madam all these years. Madam laugh Oga until shame come rub Oga face like powder. I go thief that Oga Holy Water take fight any witch wey come disturb me.

I will put on the TV and relax like my Oga and Madam. Oga and Madam would bring their heads to each other and shake it like they are small children. They would make their lips touch and then they would lick it. There is no madam here with me. Nneka is foolish. I cannot call her. But I can still imagine a madam being here oh. Wait oh, it does not have to be my own madam. The picture of my madam must not come into my head in Jesus name or I will die. My Oga can see it when he looks at me. I don't want trouble. I want to remain with Oga until he finally sends me to a technical college or even a university. Like Oga's children, I would be a big man. I would not be hungry. When I want anything, I will just deep hands into my pocket and buy a large loaf of bread and chop. I can also buy my own sardine, tease Nneka with it and make sure even a drop of oil from the can doesn't pass her by.

To be a big man is a very excellent thing. Big men put big offering in church and God blesses them with another bigger money. They walk about like big men, legs apart and hands in the air. Small road does not do them. They have big stomach too. They chop a lot. They talk big big things. They talk about big house and big problems. They marry very pretty women. Chei! I want to be a big man oh. I want to drive a big car, like Toyota Prado, like Oga. I want to stand up and talk and allow people who are not successful to sit down and talk about their poverty in silence. I want to be that big with big mouth.

Oga and Madam have gone to the airport to carry Small Madam. That pikin has been overseas since madam gave birth to her. I hear she is eighteen and she has decided to come and see Madam and Oga in this country. But My Oga did not agree when the news began oh. Oga was afraid. Afraid was catching my Oga because he had gone to pick a form in his party. He wants to be a senator. He wants to go to Abuja and become a bigger man. In Abuja, he would be closer to the President and maybe he would buy a plane then. He can't park a plane in the garage so I don't know why he would buy it sha. But my Oga does not like stress. He wants everything to happen fast fast. He does not like to stand on the line when he goes to the airport. He does not like to stand on the line in the bank. When I follow him to the bank, he would sit down and I would stand in the line until they call his name: Chief Matthias Needam! He would write his signature and he would give me the bundle of money to carry to the car. My Oga is a fine man. I like his fineness. He does not leave the house without looking at the mirror and talking fine things to himself: "I am the people's choice. Congratulations, Distinguished Senator Needam. You fought a magnificent battle."

My Oga does not like anything that makes his heart fly. If you have bad news, you go to madam and tell her. Madam would be the one to pass the message to Oga in a way that it will sweet him and not make him become sick. If Oga wants you to buy him anything and you lose your money or chop it, as the case maybe, you dare not talk to him. Bad news does not cross his gate. Big men are like that. I want to be a big man like there is no tomorrow.

Small Madam stays in America, abi na London. But all is the same. They have the same white people everywhere. I hear America is very very fine like paradise. Ah, paradise is sweet oh. When Jehovah Witness people bring their book and come show us the picture of paradise, you would want to stop bad things and wait for paradise. Animals plenty everywhere in paradise. Dem no dey even chop human being. Lion and small pikin dey play inside garden. Chei. No upstairs, no motor, people just go to anywhere on foot and they have smiles on their faces. What I don't like about it is that water easily carry people's houses and kill them in oyinbo land and that may be the same in paradise.

In the village, we had a big river but a river never left its house to another man's house to carry him and kill him and destroy his house. The rivers have respect for the people and all they do. I think that is because the people respected the river well well. They gave it eggs and hot drinks. They go and talk to the river and apologise to it when they shit inside the water or when the women mistakenly go there when their monthly visitor is around. In the village, though no light, life is very sweet. In the night we will sit around, chopping strong corn and be telling stories of tortoise and how smart he is. In the village you do not stay on the line for water. You do not wait for anybody. If your body is hot you just jump into the river and wash up. But here, hmm, it is not like that.

My Oga likes his daughter. When small madam said he would jump on a plane and come to Nigeria, Oga nearly died. He does not like talks like that. He shouted and quarrelled with madam that it is the stubborn head of madam that small madam has carried. He said that if small madam comes into Nigeria all those small small boys will come and be knocking on the door every day. He said that those mumu, who are envious of him and his new desire, will go and arrange with jobless graduates and go and kidnap his precious daughter. There is nothing he did not say to big madam but nothing worked. The more he talked the more the calls came into the telephone. Person can hear small madam shouting and screaming like say America is biting her skin comot. But small children can be very funny ehn. If I go to America today, tell me, what is that nonsense that will make me to come home? I will beg the oyinbo people to forget about my name and give me their own name. I will tell dem to forget Mene Deemua. I don't want to be called Mene again. They should call me Tomatoes or Fish. Oyinbo people have very funny names. They can call me Sardine sef. I will not mind. I will go to a place that is very fine and snap better photo and send it to the people who are here in Nigeria. When they look they will jump and appreciate Bari and tell themselves that they must leave Nigeria too. But my Oga will not send me to oyinbo land. He will make sure I wash the cars, follow him to the bank and iron his big big clothes. He would not bother me today. Hei, See Mene oh. Mene should enter a plane too and see how the other world looks like. In short, if Oga makes that mistake, I will go to America and disappear. I will not be seen again until I have become a very big man, then I will buy a bottle of Schnapps Aromatic Drink and go to tell him that though I am a bad person for running away, my mind has been paining me for all the bad things I have done against him.

Maybe he will ask me to sit down. I will sit on the leather chair in the parlour, like a fellow big man and drink whiskey with him and laugh. He will talk politics with me and tell me he likes me. He will tell me that though I ran away, he is not so angry with me, that I am still his best friend. Ha, Me? Small Mene, a best friend of a big Oga like Chief Matthias Needam? Money can make a small man the best friend of a big man oh. Once you can speak very big English and pay for your own drinks and your own cigarette you will be loved by every big man. No big man wants to buy free drinks for anybody. In short, when a big man knows that you will not pay for your own drinks, he will tell you that something has happened and that he will not come to the meeting. That is if you are a big man small oh. But some of them will not even pick your call. They will watch your call and then sigh and chew kola nut.

Small madam is really fine in the photo that madam put on the wall. She looks like a mami-water wey never sabi bad things. Madam is always proud of the picture. In the morning she will come and look at it and clean dust from it and laugh and be proud of herself. I like that. When I grow up too, and have money as a big man and marry a wife, I will have a daughter that will be as fine as small madam and I will train her abroad. I will send her to Imperial College, yes that is the place where Oga said he took small madam to. I will hang my daughter's photo in the parlour too and tell my friends about her school fees and how big it is. I will finish training her and when she wants to get married I will make sure she marry another big man. Yes naw. Big men do not marry small men. When a big man get pikin, he will train her so that the poor man will not have the mind to approach her and say anything to her. In short, the only place they can meet is the church. But a big man can decide to use police inside the church and God no go vex. God does not vex for big men. They build the house of God. They can hire police men to stand in church and watch the eyes of the people who will look in the direction of their daughters. I will be like that. I will have twenty police men. I will make two walk with my daughter every day. Ten will walk with me. Three will be at home. Five will be with my wife. All that will happen in our house will smell of police. Mosquito will be very afraid to even fly in my house. I will not hire somebody like yeye Johnbull who will sleep and forget that he is a gateman. When Oga comes he would be shouting so much and the mumu will not even wake up. I would be the one to run from the house and open his gate for him. But at the end of the month, he will be the first to stop Oga when he wants to enter motor and ask for his salary.

But me, I like Johnbull. He has heart. He can meet anyone and ask for anything. I am very afraid and shy. I cannot even meet Lemene and ask for her hands for friendship. In the streets, people who are small, people who I am taller than, have girlfriends and I do not have. I do not have, not because I do not bother oh. It is because I do not have heart, the heart to tell a girl that this is what I feel inside my heart and that it is very unique.

Lemene is a fine girl. She is Chief Ikoma's daughter. Chief Ikoma is not a proper chief oh. He calls himself chief. And everybody calls him chief also. He has a big cloth with lion head that he wears. I do not like him. It is Lemene that I love. When you see Lemene's smooth legs, you will shout for Jesus to come down and forget about heaven and his father's kingdom. Lemene is so beautiful that when people come to buy garri from them they drop change and never collect it back. They stammer and become like mumu. I love Lemene. I am not a mumu for her oh, but if she asks me to be a mumu, I will go inside the house, bath and rub very fine cream with fine aroma and become her mumu.

It is almost night. Oga has not come back. Madam has not come back too. I don't want trouble. I don't want to go to the bed in my room and sleep. I want to sleep in the parlour, on this leather chair. They will wake me when they come. Oga will shout and I will wake up. If I do not, Nneka can be the new Mene for today. As for me, let me be the alternate Oga small.

27

A PEOPLE OF THE RIVER

A PEOPLE OF THE RIVER

Kwame stepped out of the hut in one of his old school shorts, his head buried in admiration for the khaki, how it seemed, with time, to fit his waist more than ever. It was his first pair of shorts. He received it when he joined the primary school. Today, he had more than five. But this one is special. It was the first piece of cloth he wore the day he lost trust for his mother. Nothing really special, he had been enrolled in school without his knowledge and one day, the woman brought home a slate which had the English alphabet printed in front while the back was blank. The smiling woman handed him the gift and unwrapped a pair of shorts, the ones he wore. Although, when it first came, the two ripped spots behind it were not there and the colour was a thicker kind of blue, not the fading tone it had washed down to. And as for how he lost trust for his mother, she had taken him to school and made him admire the school compound and showed him his classroom. She told him that she had to return to get the snacks she forgot to buy. All effort to join her in getting the forgotten snacks was abortive, and that was how the woman didn't return to school. Other forms of tricks made him give up on trust.

"You could learn to tie wrapper sometimes", his father spoke in the local language. "Men tie wrapper when they have somewhere important to go to." Kwame didn't lift his head up when he responded that they were not going to any important function but a small fishing trip, one which serves as his first, an introduction to a trade he would soon take up, as a man, someone who would be a breadwinner someday, someone whose sisters would have to call on when they have issues in their husbands' houses. He would be the one to order for a meeting when there was quarrel in the compound or when something important was to take place.

"A meeting with nature is important. God is in nature. In fact, God is super nature. The Rivers and the seas are means to him. When meeting them for a favour, it is expected that you dress importantly, and for us in this part of the world, a piece of wrapper around the waist, firmly tied, is necessary. But you are a boy, a boy who is a man. A first born male child is a man from birth. Responsibilities await his growth."

Kwame returned to the hut and reappeared in a wrapper. The old man looked at him and produced a smile. "Saro Nwineedam, this looks more like it." Kwame maintained his indifferent look and retouched the edge of the wrapper where a lump was formed. He picked a cut jerry can while his father stood and faced the sun, determining the position of the river. He scooped a handful of sand and threw it in the air. If it flowed with the wind to the west, the river was forming and it would be full. If it flowed to the east, it would be dry and good for a catch. The sand flew to the west and the old man stood for a while, undecided. And then like a child awoken with a pinch, he walked towards the river. Kwame followed.

His paddle held over his shoulder, the old man led the way. If he had made a quicker step he would have stepped on the black cat which crossed from his right to his left. At first, it didn't occur to him what had happened but when his paddle fell down, its arrowed part missing his foot by a tiny inch, the old man shook his head and said it wasn't a good one. If he was 20 or 30 or 40 or 50 he would run back home heaving heavily about the signs, but he was a man who had seen countless Christmas celebrations by the new church. He was the same man who had thrown broken pieces of kola nut to his zim at the side of the hut which served as sitting room.

Kwame, unconcerned with his father's thoughts, looked around, admiring healthy maize cubs which were brightly green. His eyes trailed a bird which landed on one of the flowers of the maize and pecked. He picked up a stone and threw at it. He missed but the sound reached his father and the old man turned but didn't say a word. When he had walked a distance, the old man almost talking to himself said, a man who was chasing after an elephant had no business with crickets.

The river was full to its brim when Kwame and his father got there. The canoe was already floating within bounds. Kwame held the paddle while his father untied the boat from a stake. He drew it to the tail of the river and Kwame dropped his burden in it. He climbed over. It was not his first time. He was a boy and friends with other boys. On some of those days no one found him anywhere around the house, it was fishing that he went to, with friends.

The old man paddled gently and the river took the boat smoothly. It flowed far away from land. The grove grew closer and the old man pointed at the spot where they would fish. There, if they concentrated with a net, they could make good catch. They sailed gradually to the spot and the old man asked Kwame to take up the net and cast. He had come to learn but he had not expected it would be the first thing he would do on this trip. Maybe he would have done better with clearing the net of caught fish and unwanted particles but he didn't object. He held the net and threw it. When he dragged it out with all his strength it caught five small fishes and two bigger ones. His father's nod said a lot. He threw it again and caught three bigger fishes and no smaller one. His joy could not be contained. He looked at the old man and he held his shoulder. "You will make a great fisherman." The old man paused and examined his boy's vigour. "You should take care of your mother. You are a man now. You can throw net and catch fish. When you add a little age you shall find a wife too—women are like fish in the water—to get the best you have to be diligent."

Kwame might have nodded but it wasn't because he understood the old man. He affirmed because that was what kids do when adults talk to them so the adults don't look ridiculous.

When Kwame threw the net for the third time he noticed that a heavy object dropped into the river. He turned to confirm but the old man was gone and the river was calm like nothing dropped inside.

Kwame must have stared at the spot forever when he heard a scream. Someone was rowing towards him. "My father, he is in here. He dropped inside" and between disbelief and grief Kwame shook uncontrollably. "We are all of the river. Your father has gone home. You walked him home. He had walked his own father home and his father, the father before his father. This river is our beginning and our end. Its flow represents our going and coming. You are a man, Kwame."

BIRTH

BIRTH

When Uzodimma was born, it was pure joy. The heavens wore a new look. The clouds wore colourful head-ties and sang and danced and poked each other. The joy that rented the air was as pure as Mama's smacking of her tongue each time she was sold a fresh bottle of original honey at the Peace Motor Park, Nsukka, on our way to Enugu on a weekend for her maternity hangout. Mama would dip a finger into the thick honey and let drops of it slide down her tongue then she would gaze into the open, like she was communing with the god of taste, the one who authenticated all things and gave its feedback. Mama would smile and nod and say in Igbo that this one had passed the first test, the tongue-test. Then she would ask for a box of matches. The young seller would frantically ask around for a box and hand it over to her for the final judgement. She would push the box open, pick a stick and dip the brown head inside the honey and strike it. If it lit despite the dripping honey, it was pure and original.

But when Uzo's arrival was announced through madam Ifeoma, the heavy one who wheeled a barrow load of okpa through the junior staff quarters every morning, screaming 'Okpa di oku', joy unprintable seized my face and that of Ife who was getting to understand humans and what it was that drive us crazy. Nsukka could be dry. And the rare baby wind which visited each time it was bored would not spare the red dust some relaxation. It raised it and dashed it against our white shorts. "In the north, it picked up humans and tossed them wherever it pleased" Nze would say. Nze grew up in Kano. "It was the medicine that our ancestors made that limited the baby wind around Nsukka," Ekene would conclude with a mischievous laughter. He was six and a half years my senior but I was taller. And one would not notice the stain on the dresses until the clothes were soaked. We were in one of these white dresses, white shorts and singlet for me and only shorts for Ife, papa's preference, building a car with woods, when the ultimate message came. "A child is born!" Madam Ifeoma threw the good news on the floor, unmindful whether it is breakable. We heard Madam Ifeoma from the backyard and leaped for joy. Our joy was not particularly like that of every member of the house. I mean, it was, but our own joy, the one Ife and I shared was just not the one the family celebrated. For Papa, another boy had arrived. It was a big celebration. He had three. If he grew older and died, it would not be a mean funeral. It would be that of a man who in his time sired three male children. That was the joy of the house. Madam Ifeoma would get free drinks and food. She'd sing and get sprayed with money like she did when Ife was born. But the joy I shared with Ife was slightly different, though connected to the same source. In our happiness, there was no male or female. In short, it was useless as far as we were concerned.

This is how Ife became a part of the plan. When he could talk, I took him by the hand to the backyard and showed him empty tins of milk and Bournvita that papa bought when he was born. 'Mama does not like sugar,' I told him. 'Through persuasion, she would sometimes take tea and few slices of bread in the morning. A week or two could pass and she would not return to the provision. That was where I made my first mark.' I told Ife how I strolled into the room, to watch mother and the new Ife, and perched around the edge of the bed where she arranged the provision. She paid me little attention. When I was done with whatever job she had for me, I would politely open one of the tins, smile at Mama and scoop a spoonful of milk into my mouth. Once I talked through a mouthful of milk and it went down the wrong track, my eyes welled water and Mama asked me to take it easy, 'Were ya nwayo, nwa m.' Ife counted the tins of provisions and they were thirteen. Maybe this child would need more. Maybe we would get more from his arrival. Maybe his luck would be that we opened a store house of milk and Bournvita.

HOW TO SAY GOODBYE

HOW TO SAY GOODBYE

When Zasi stepped into the lush showroom, the cool, the fragrance, the well lit lights, the welcoming display screen showing how perfectness is achieved at last, made her drop the lump of complaint which hung somewhere around her throat, ready for the right listener. Soft tunes from a hidden speaker reeled out what was left of Christy Lane's One Day at a Time; a song she practically grew up with. Her mum liked it so much she played it very early in the morning until she left for school. At a point, she felt Christy was someone from within her neighbourhood—a distant white lady who she might have met during a morning walk to school. But the air-conditioner in the shop had the best of her, sending lust signal from her exposed ankle to her neck then her head—undressing her slenderness.

Why shop owners put up such doors, such that require one's blood to push, is still a shocker to her. If she had relented in her push, the door would have sprang backward, sending her crashing into the car she had borrowed from home. What happens to one of those fancy doors which spreads open, like Jesus' arms at the cathedral, when a customer approaches? But thoughts are better sealed in foreign environments, Zasi concluded.

On the side where she started, they were more expensive. Or so. No prices were on them but they looked luxurious—gold plaited. They had some fine gold crests, two on top and some around the base. And they sparkled in the light. They looked like the ones she had seen on TV, the ones which made her visit the shop, used by the very wealthy.

Zasi ran her hand over the steel base and around the golden handle by the side. This handle, this sleek one she touched, was placed to make it easier for lifting. But how many persons could lift it using the handle, she thought. Zasi turned around and saw a frail man, bulge eyed, neatly dressed and with an appreciable smile. His tie stretched properly like it was starched and ironed. He asked, almost solemnly, if she wanted the ones on the platform where she stood, or the ones over another platform, pointing a distance away, where they were more elegant and creatively designed without gold. And his voice, a salesman's priceless possession, shrill, did a piece of magic—for she closed her eyes and leaned forward, with her lips—in her mind.

Over there, where he pointed was a haven of beauties. From where she stood, though transfixed, she could see herself being magically drawn to stand before these boxes of affluence. If they were small, if they could fit into her D&G purse, she'd love to carry them around and maybe set them at a table, in front of Mabel and gossip about a beauty she had decided to grace her eventual departure with.

Were they made here? She asked. With some unforced laughter or a giggle or anything but loud laugher, the frail one responded. They were not made in Nigeria but coupled here. Zasi closed her eyes, sucked in the fine fragrance of the shop; her known souvenir, and reached forth her hand like a child in a quest to be carried up by a loved one, and she could touch them, just that she hadn't moved an inch closer yet.

You're sure you don't want to go closer? The voice woke her. She wanted to go closer and touch it all around. If it wouldn't be weird, she would love to take a brief selfie with it or maybe pose inside the one with the emblem of a miniature Christ. She walked closer and touched the few she could and just couldn't stop wondering how this shop had so much splendour, not for the regular but the very wealthy who, like the very poor, would eventually make the great trek from consciousness.

What kind of casket are you looking for, ma'am? Nothing particularly expensive, she said. It is not like if I lay in it I would find healing or wake up somewhere finer, she thought.

Is it for a loved one? The man asked, sizing her. And for once, the question forestalled her thoughts. Actually, it was for her but she had not had it in her mind that she was going to die. Yes, she would die. The papers said so. The doctor wrote it a week ago. She should be in bed, resting. But why perfume a dead rat?, she screamed before going shopping. She had to make sure she did for herself the things she couldn't do all the while. She had gone to the florist for a beautiful bouquet. She wanted a touch of purple. And she wanted the place where she would lie in state to be sprinkled with roses. She loved roses and the letter she concluded last night had strict instructions for her interment.

When Adams first gave her roses, she knew she had to love him. But no one should love a man just because he gave that which they desired. Somehow, she and Adams drifted apart and maybe it was great. Maybe fate worked it out. If he was around and learned of the cancer, he might have been broken beyond repair. He was a frail man, like this one who sold caskets. But in his frailness he didn't count his words. He spoke confidently. And his choice of words was impeccable. They could have been especially preselected and transmitted to him each time he was to use them. But words too fail. Adams' words at some point became regular. She could guess his vocabulary, the delivery, of a man she had known for six months. The accent, if she closed her eyes, made her want to find the speaker and place a kiss on his lips but that, the urge to kiss anyone, was gone too until the frail one spoke.

She was numb, in heart and loving. Maybe loving the job of shopping for her funeral worked. Maybe that was the ultimate. Maybe that should have been her career. Not a nurse. Not the constant sight of blood, of men who could not pay bills. Her choice of a hospital, the one that helped the downtrodden, was great but unwise, to her desires.

Zasi gave the frail one a card and it went into a machine. The deliverer would have it sent to the given location, her home address, in an hour or less, the man said. If the Port Harcourt traffic lessened it would arrive in time for her to reveal her status to her Mum, Dornu and Suanu, her twin.

DEADNESS

DEADNESS

How did Tuabia Kagbaranee become the one who held the heart of Pyagbara Gbenekanu in her palm firmly? That story has to be told so there would be clarity to what a pretty face can achieve.

You know, back then in junior secondary school, the teacher, with chalk stained fingers, would point at the prettiest girl in the class, the one seated at the back of the room and ask her to stand up. And she, induced in the act of chewing gum, would smack her lips, size the teacher from head to toe and adjust her pinafore and then move her body mildly to the astonishment of the boys who watched from every corner of the room and then strain an ear to hear her latest accusation. And the teacher would shake her head and say that a pretty face is facade, that it would lead no one anywhere. But that could have been grossly thought in the negative because everyone with a pretty face controls everyone with a pretty pocket.

And that was how it happened, that when Pyagbara returned from the United States, with the many bags which took two lorries to be carried into his old father's zinc house, and he stepped outside the epic mess that he left behind ten years ago, he shook his head disapprovingly to Bari for his negligence of his family. He used his eyes to measure the length of space that could fit a small storey building, a small haven he would give his father as a token for his patience all these years and as consolation for the loss of his wife, his mother, the woman in whose arms this frail old man looked like a soldier; full of life and never tired of helping on the farm.

Anyway, it was this man, the returnee, caring, purposeful and calculative who walked into the hands of Tuabia who had just left the house of one of his toy boys. When she saw him, his sneakers still shiny and his heavy clothes despite the sun, his earring sparkling in Dukana's sun, she knew that this one, like a couple of others she had seen, was a returnee who had brought home dollars to be sucked, absorbed and carefully silenced. She winked at him and adjusted the melons on her chest and that moment marked the beginning of the last moment Pyagbara Gbenekanu owned his senses again.

Pyagbara stayed home for two months and spent one hundred percent of his stay between the thighs of Tuabia, pounding and digging for things only him knew how valuable they were. His old man called for meetings and invited the village seer but the old seer saw nothing, just interlocked hearts, so strong, binding two semi-young people everlastingly.

The space for the erection of the new house he marked with his eyes remained untouched. The roof which leaked on the first night he returned home to pick his clutch bag, the one which contained dollars, remained unchanged. And so it was observed that his ten years savings went into beautifying a modern day beauty salon for Tuabia and buying her a Volkswagen salon car with customised wheels. And one day, Tuabia sighted another richer returnee and changed the locks of her apartment. And Pyagbara, clutching his madness and a pair of whatever that was left on him as trousers, found his way into his old man's leaking hut on a rainy day and perched like a chicken that had been in the rain, one that had stubbornly gone out and become drenched against all admonition to stay sane. And his old man who nodded to every apology he offered slept for the last time that night.

SLUM DIARY

SLUM DIARY

Click! It comes twice. The first click may have a flash. But the second click surely does. The flash light comes blinding. But that isn't my problem. I like it, especially when I'm placed on serious smiles with crisp notes. Halima, that woman I love, likes it when I smile. Other children envy me. I can't tell why that is so, but my curly hair, my skin colour, and my stature are mainly part of the speculations.

The white men that visit Bori always find us fascinating. They enjoy all we do. From clicking at children diving into streams, to sweating teenagers cleaning the windscreen of cars for money, they love all we do. A lot of them wouldn't buy what we sell. But they would never any pictures. They would click at cats crossing the road. They would click at quarreling market women and struggling bus conductors. They also click at monuments. You see them in armed vehicles. Someone said taking pictures of us was a good thing. He said the pictures travel to the white lands and is put on large billboards and computers. And it makes us famous. Others have said the pictures generate funds for these people. When I heard that I intensified my charge for every picture snapped.

When I grow up I want to have many children, maybe ten or fifteen of them. And I would position them around the country with large bowls like the one I have now. I would take some to Port Harcourt, I heard the people there are rich. Someone said there is oil money everywhere, even in the air, especially in Bonny, an Island close to the Garden City, where women go for good luck, and beggars like us go for mercies. I would take a half of my children there and make them bug all the white and black people so one day we would pool resources and build ourselves a big house. I am sure the dream would be achieved. I would send a couple of them to Lagos. The governor stopped us from hawking and trading on the street. He stopped our business. He stopped everything because he knows nothing and cares little. That is bad business. He wants to kill my dreams.

I would have made so much money today if I had been discovered by another white tourist. But I didn't. I missed my luck. I was at the National Stadium where the President's daughter celebrated her eighteenth birthday. The nation gathered. And I found enough food to last me the day.

Tomorrow is another day. Maybe I would find my dearest, Halima, and tell her of my dreams of ten or fifteen children and the business idea I thought up. I like Halima a lot. I have not told her, because I think I am not ready yet. I will be fifteen in a month. Maybe I will add some height. Someone said I won't grow any taller. I know it's a lie, I will grow taller and marry Halima and have so much money and maybe have a family snap shot from the click of the camera of one of the tourists.

THE FLIGHT

THE FLIGHT

Dele and Lewuga strolled outside the house with the big cherry tree nonchalantly. If a stranger saw them, he would see two innocent children who may not be more than 12, in school uniforms, calculating how they would get home or attend to their assignments. But someone who knew Victoria Street very well and knew Dele and Lewuga would tell you that the two boys, who were actually 10 but looked bigger, could not stroll around the compound of anyone who didn't have something to lose. Dele and Lewuga felt fruits a second before they were fully ripe. They arrived to hunt it the moment the fruit was ripe. Many times, the fruit became ripe in their rooms.

The cherry tree outside the big white house had history. The year before last year, a certain couple had brought a bowl at night. And while the wife picked, the husband climbed the tree and held the branch with more fruit, shaking until the sound of falling cherries couldn't be distinguished from the sound of heavy rainfall. But it was not the season of rain and when such sound came on, the neighbourhood panicked. The man who owned the cherry woke up, picked his gun and fired a shot. There was scuttling and the abandonment of a bowl. The next day it was in the news that a certain Dumka Aminikpo had broken his leg. An angry antelope had chased him. His wife boiled water and nursed him.

Last year, two young men who operated the machine that ground garri in the village took a cue from the unsuccessful couple and visited the cherry at night and climbed up with a bag. They plucked so much, noiselessly and filled their bags. When they climbed down and gave each other hi-fives, the other chuckle they heard was not theirs but that of an old man who stood at the end of a double-barrel gun which aimed at them. They dropped the bags and no one saw them for two weeks. When they appeared, with marks of cane on their bodies they said they had gone to the next village to help the youths prepare for their forthcoming masquerade festival.

Dele and Lewuga had heard stories about the precision of the man in the white house. And besides, the tree had red and other coloured wrappers pinned at the base of the tree—an imported medicine bought from Oron to catch thieves and keep them until morning. It was rumoured that whoever climbed would be stuck there. But Dele and Lewuga didn't bother. Their mission was not to climb but to know if the man was around—they feared no voodoo, just the barrel of a gun.

While they strolled, they looked at the garage and places where one could hide and spy on someone on the tree. When it seemed the coast was clear, Dele quickly raced up the tree and before he could catch his own breath his bag was full. Lewuga went to a corner and scooped a bowl size of sand and dropped at the bottom of the tree and told the medicine that if it could finish counting the sand before it was dark it could kill them. And they smiled.

When they picked their filled bags, the big bang they heard was not of firecracker but a gunshot which missed Dele's leg by sheer luck. It was the old man, lying beneath his Peugeot 504. Dele and Lewuga dropped the bags and flew. And when they stopped to catch their breath, unknown to them, it was within range from the old man's shot that they squatted, recalling what had happened.

LIKE FILTERED CIGARETTE

LIKE FILTERED CIGARETTE

On his way back from class, his bag flung over his shoulder and his head slightly bent like someone punished and warned against looking at faces. Alfred walked home quietly, counting footfalls and deep in thought, not of something heavy but a bit important, something that may happen but currently looked unthinkable. Would he at a point in his life summon enough courage to walk into the house of the parents of any girl to ask for their daughter's hand in marriage? How would he initiate the conversation? Maybe the girl would have done some preliminary works and introduced him:

"Hi, dad and mum. You guys remember Alfred from the phone, the one who calls at nine every night? He would be coming over to see you guys soon."

And maybe with her smile her parents would ask of what honour was a caller's visit and maybe they would agree it was just an innocent visit. But, you know, money changes everything. If a young man was done with school and landed a juicy job with the right benefits, wouldn't that too be a morale booster? Maybe he wouldn't be timid after all and his stammering wouldn't mean a thing because they would sip from an expensive bottle of wine and laugh more and shake hands.

Alfred counted his steps not to keep records for any experiment, it was rather one way he didn't care to think about the distance from the department to his home. It was a 30-minute walk through cars and sometimes groups of students who talked loudly or those who hung around any spot that had better Internet signal. It could be about a thousand steps but he had never counted it. Sometimes he counted 10 or

50 and missed it and stopped or he would just stare at his own feet, how they succeeded each other in walks, not stepping on the other, as if they had eyes.

Alfred's count helped him keep calm and composed. Thoughts rushed to his head when he walked home and only some counting or humming of a song distracted his memories. He was on this road a month and ten days ago when his phone beeped. The SMS had said, "We need to talk" and impatiently, he dialled her number and she told him that she was leaving. She couldn't continue with him, a 30 year old who was an overstay student of a 5 years course. When his phone dropped, he too dropped but quickly rose and walked to a corner, under a small tree, where sat in deep thought until it was 9pm, until his phone alarm for reading jerked him back to reality.

He was devoted to Chioma, his girlfriend. She was pretty with thin nose and small eyes which made her vision better at night when they read together. When she wore hairstyles it was cornrows. Sometimes he joked that she was a Deeper Lifer, for though she wore trousers her hairstyle was typical of that religious sect which preached modesty. And Chioma, that's not her actual name, but the name he chose for her for it was a beautiful name—Good God—wasn't such a God who made such a slender lady good? The sound of the name—how it wrapped around the mouth like good meal—it was his favourite Igbo name as she was his favourite Igbo lady. But each day he went to school and saw the new faces that were either freshly admitted or were from another department, he feared that one day this lady he loved may become estranged from him, for no one loved to be shared with anyone. If he wasn't at fault, her lover would be the one to leave, for he felt it strongly when he made to be introduced to the fresh students.

But estrange, why does it exists, that people who once knew each other closely would lose themselves and maybe never speak with them again. And they would wipe their numbers off their phones so when they called it would be ordinary like every other numbers, unregistered and strange and due for scrutiny, but if love didn't die honourably and maybe a thing lived beneath the estrangement, when a call came through, at the first "hello" and "hi" the caller would be identified.

Alfred heard his name and turned. The voice was Chioma's but the caller was not there. He answered and walked towards the direction it called from. He walked until it was the endless bush-path that he covered. And when he was found wandering deeper four days later by someone who suspected he was a student of the university, his clothes were not on him. What covered his loins from the glaring eyes of the public was absolutely nothing. Though he maintained an unending smile and calm, his rescuer shook his head and said this one, like those he read in books had lost his mind to wandering spirits of the forest dressed as love.

WHAT DEATH BRINGS

WHAT DEATH BRINGS

How do you look at the person you loved in the morgue, stretched out and blank to the realities of man's worries? Eyelids sealed and lips shut never to be opened. Nudeness covered by a piece of wrapper—the one your mum pulled off her waist when labour pains began and you panicked but was reassured that it was normal. For though shame is homeless in the body, saneness can only be said of the attendant if what was once respected is treated as though it was still very much respected, so when someone came to see another person, what they saw wasn't another, another man's wife, who was stretched, wasted and uncovered so that when the visitor returned home he would say: ah, today I saw what death brings, total nothingness to man's treasures for what I saw could not have seen if one didn't die and was kept in a morgue.

The hands that once held yours firmly before youth service, same that you kissed and spoke to, that whatever it took, when service to motherland was done, it would be on one of the fine fingers of the held hands that a ring; your own special gift, not for her, necessarily, but a symbol of the commitment you owe her love and the precious moments you shared together, that same hands were same that lay withered on the mat that was bed.

Spirit detached, unavailable, hanging somewhere, watching the dress of a body that it once wore for many years, from babyhood to maturity. How do you do it? How do you keep calm and stare and hope that though this is reality, it should be a reality in the movie so when end-credit rolled, it would be the beginning of a process that was only fictional? And deadness could pack its burden and leave and you, the one who has lost someone to death's insatiability, you would walk to the mat that was bed, lift the once dead lady into your arms, hug and kiss her, and promise to never leave her again because she, like Christ, has conquered death.

You met her on a cold Sunday evening on campus, on your way to Hilltop to bind an assignment. You wrapped your hands around your body and when she saw you, she asked if you were okay. It was the way she showed interest, the way she spoke with you until you arrived at the shop that made you ask for a second meeting and another one after the second. You worshipped at St. Peters' because you wanted to sit next to her, to feel her fragrance. And even when you mixed up the words during mass, you did not care much, for each time the words were mixed up, she smiled at you and you felt alright.

How do you unhide your eyes and turn it to that which had been an inseparable part of you, lying in stillness? How do you do it? How do you summon courage to stand before the one you had made a promise, to be there at sunrise and sunset and on cloudy days when darkness unseats daylight? She was the one you told that when war rages, you two, side by side, faith by faith, would stand against odds and fight and win and celebrate so when people come, those who would come after your reign on earth, they would know that no mean couple walked this path?

Do you throw out your shoes, fold the sleeves of your shirt, lie next to this better half and wish that the spirits which led you two to each other would take both your hands, the dead and the living, and bond them and take you two on that journey to lovingness eternal?

Do you walk confidently behind the morgue attendant with your hand folded to the back, fingers interlocked and palm sweaty, because this is not how you imagined it would end? You had buried the stillborn and would do same to the mother? How do you breathe? What do you breathe? Do you breath air filtered of love? How does your heart beat?

That you once held this lifeless body and smiled with her and looked into her eyes and cupped her face in your hands when shyness won't let her continue looking at you that day at Vet Hills. And when you ended the sweet lines you had given to her like a poem, you lifted her head and kissed her lips. How do you stand before this body and express your regret that you couldn't do much to save her, though you donated the blood the hospital requested?

How do you apologise that if you knew that the birth of a child would bring about such complications, you would have decided to live with her singly and happily, with no thought of a child? The plan, that you two would travel the world, make jokes and write tiny words on pieces of papers and stick them on your dresses, words that described how priceless you guys were to each other. But they are the things you will never get to do. They would go into the list of the things you would love to present to God, so while he prepares you for a next life, they will be among the first to be considered.

But God, yes, God, where has He been? How does he watch from his throne as the world is thrown in madness, of a once loved man turns lovelorn, of a young family with dreams stripped of tangibility and given emptiness? She called you "Isi Okpa" and you called her "Iru Abacha." What amuses him, God, the foolery of man, of where he is when he should be elsewhere, what he ought to do and what he never gets to know? What tickles Him, the unknowingness of his day of death, so everyday he wakes up he is on death row, because he is made for the pleasure of God and he has no opinion about his own life?

How do you stop to think and live when a casket sinks, the one that has her? Shouldn't it sink your sorrow too as it has taken your pride? Shouldn't it take your thought of ending your own existence as soon as the mourners return to their homes? Shouldn't the dug sand blink and say they understand your pains and would be there when you, like the beauty in the grave, would lie covered in the coolness of their arms? Shouldn't the air stop at what death brings and the sun take a long nap forever?

IN THE DARK

IN THE DARK

The five bikers you approached smelt of gin and filth. When the sixth man requested for your destination, the stench from his mouth and body gagged your breath. Like Christopher, he could have had a jar of the local gin that afternoon. You walked away, disappointed, to a man who sat leaning on a mango tree with his face covered in what looked like a face-cap. You tapped him and he jumped to his feet like he had been prompted to challenge an enemy. You calmed him and explained that you needed his services. He searched his cloth and returned with a key. He turned his ignition and all you heard was a pathetic cough. He gestured for a push and you reluctantly helped. He smelt sane.

Bewildered, you examined the rickety motorbike whose seat seemed inconsiderately chopped by some antagonising spirits. It moved like an old woman but with unlimited smoke. The biker screamed in his native language for you to jump. You grudgingly contemplated. When you delayed, he remarked about your feminine frame. You climbed when the stare increased.

You swallowed a keg of saliva each time his speed doubled. You wished you had prayed, but God had ceased to exist in your life two years ago, when you left the university.

You had to see your mother. Life had been uneasy since you left her. The village would have had you lynched if you had not sneaked out through her kitchen window. The youths arrived that night for your head. They had caught you with Nwigbo, the carpenter. You held his large work table while he took you to paradise from behind. Your father, who you hated the most, not for his coldness but closed heart, died a year and a half ago. Three years, painful but worth it, had gone. Transformed, at least physically from working out, you don't know how your mother would look at you. Wrinkles are heartless, they might have rented her face and given her less attractive smiles, you thought. But a smile, no matter the sadness, always comes out refined. You wished her everything good and tried to contain your thoughts.

The path to your community had not changed. Overgrown grasses still decorated the way. A few scanty electric poles stood lonely, with connecting cables. They were the only change you noticed. Maybe if you cared much, the carpeted coal tar would have mattered. But they were just there, unnoticeable. You tried to feel the rushing wind which poured into your face like a welcome gesture but you felt uneasy, heavy with words in your head for your mother. Would she scream when she heard of your partnership with Chris? You looked ahead, to endless possibilities.

The man in front of you kept a straight head on the road. The wind made his shirt fatter as he sped. The fat shirt rose like a troubled lump of flesh and you smelled his poverty.

The okada reached the junction where you had to point him to your mother's home. And when he made the turn, your mother's hut was just in front of you. The mud wall had cracks in it. The door hung on one hinge, like a symbol of the wrongness of poverty. Some thatches were displaced. And you saw the window, the same one that saved your miserable life. You stared at the open hole; it was the only source of light that complimented the door. You heard nothing. The okada man stretched out a hand for his money, unmindful of your recollections. You found him a piece of the many naira notes in your pocket. He made to go and you screamed at him for the change. He frantically tried to please you with apologies. You collected your money and folded your slightly giant body into the hut. The smell of burnt firewood hit your large, flat nose. You dusted stains from the door off your pink shirt and tried to find a figure in the dark room.

You saw nobody. Not even the lizards you played with when you were younger. Then you looked at the fireplace where the smoke had its headquarters. You saw a body next to the fire, befriending the heat. You greeted her lowly, like she was a deity. She made a smile that could be seen in the dark, same as you had imagined. You asked her a billion questions about her health and she ignored them to ask of your education. Slender, her image seemed muddled up with a shadow. When you thought her questions were over she dropped a deafening yet troubled request.

"I want a grandchild, Kenule."

You heaved, settled on the mat where she lay and unpacked your bag. You dropped a tin of milk, a loaf of bread and some multivitamins by her side. She pushed them away gradually, like an old woman adjusting a sleeping child.

"Girls from this village make good wives."

Her words concluded like a last wish and you tried to extrapolate. You made to fetch some water from the clay pot blackened by age but she held back your spirit with a call.

"Kenule, hope you changed."

She struggled to hold invisible objects for support, to look at your shaved face and the well-trimmed beard while you watched baby fire pick feeble hands and rest on smoking firewood. Each progress of the building fire reminded you of childhood, how you placed maize and pear next to a red coal to make a meal. Then silence ensued. Your mother gave up the attempt to rise. She stayed calm, breathed like a baby. And your mind leapt. You stood up to inquire if it was a goodbye message but her eyes livened at yours, and for the first time since you arrived, the picture of Christopher popped into your head, his lips and how they tasted like peppermint.

IN ADAMS' DREAM

IN ADAMS' DREAM

Once upon a time there was a boy who could not talk. He lived with his grandmother after his mother left him for the city. She left him to look for a job so he could go to school like his friends.

Daily, when Adams' grandmother went to the farm, he would follow her. He carried the hoe and a tiny bottle of water for himself. When the sun became too uncomfortable, he would sip some of the water. He was such a dedicated boy.

One day Adams fell ill. Grandmother had planned to harvest some cassava. She requested that Adams stay at home and take his medications but Adams was too attached to grandma to allow her go alone to the distant farmland.

Adams leaped from his bed. He struggled towards the place he had kept the hoe since the previous time they went to the farm. He carried it over his shoulder and went outside to wait for his grandmother.

At the farm, Adams' temperature rose. He sat under a shade and hummed a song. It was a song his mother sang to him when she would want him to catch some sleep. As Adams hummed, he fell asleep.

In Adams' dream, he was a pupil at one of the most prestigious schools in the city. He wore a colourful, well pressed shirt and a pair of shorts. His socks sparkled in the sunlit day. His sandals looked well polished. He had alighted from a luxury car, such that had many tyres. He waved at the driver and walked to meet his friends. Then a voice called from a distance. When he turned, he woke up. The large shadow of his grandmother stood over him.

"I told you to stay home, Adams."

"But who would have looked after you, grandma?" he thought. And grandma saw a response in his eyes.

"God. He always takes care of me, you must know."

"How come I never see him walk you to the farm?" Adams thought.

"I see him, son. I see him daily."

"How come I don't see him, grandma?" He questioned with his eyes.

"That's because He walks inside of you, son. You are my protector. See how you insisted on taking me to the farm even when you are unfit? Isn't that God?"

Adams' eyes beamed excitement. He thought for a while. He looked at grandma and the green plants all around him. They danced and nodded in agreement to grandma's words.

When Adams got home he met a surprise. His mum was back. She had returned to take him to the city so he could go to school and maybe wear sparkling socks and well pressed shirts and shorts.

WORLD PEOPLE

WORLD PEOPLE

When my own chicken pox visited, it was unannounced. The day had begun blankly. There was no early morning rainfall such that would raise my body temperature. No one had seen a black cat crisscrossing the pathway to our house. Mama had not announced that she had kicked her left foot against a large stone the previous day or had any of the four prayer warriors from the church come to forewarn us of impending danger on a family member. I had not dreamt of any fierce looking masquerade chasing me either. I woke up early, blocked the ray of the sun that peeped through the space between the door and its hinges. I tapped Lezua's leg and when he would not stop turning without waking up, I kicked him hard. When his eyes opened at me, bloodshot, he acted like someone who swallowed something bitter. Lezua would not touch me. If he did, it would be a bad day. I would scream down the entire compound and every parent would want to know what demon he had dined with in his dream to inflict such grave pain on an outwardly reserved child like Nia.

It was a normal Deemua. The sun had woken up as usual, done the usual lightening up of the earth, and people like Lezua and I had stood before it to stretch our bodies in its warmth. It was also in this early morning sun that displeased parents stood to lay curses on stubborn children who would neither help them on the farm nor go to school like others. Mama never did that. Though once, when she was accused of stealing a hoe in the compound, to clear her name of the accusation, mama had dropped her wrapper in the face of the morning sun and sworn her innocence and invoked the wrath of Yor Naayon, the deity of thunder, to vindicate her. It was intense and no one blamed her again.

The day before its arrival, Lezua and I went to the stream against the instruction of mama. We sneaked out while she was peeling cassava. We were dirty, we told her. We had just returned from the farm where we had gone to uproot cassava. Though my job was to watch the environment for any strange faces, I was the one who gathered the uprooted cassava. I did it with my entire body. I arranged the cassavas in a small heap of eight or nine tubers and when I could not carry them with hands apart, I lay them on my belly to the spot where the larger heap was placed.

Lezua, like mama, uprooted the cassavas. I was barred from uprooting. When I did, I left some in the ground. I didn't know the process of locating the cassava using the roots. Mama had said all that in one swift breath in K'ana and I understood her. I gathered Lezua's and Mama's into three sections. When the process was over, or when we had nagged about spending so much time on the farm, Mama used her machete to scrub against the hoe, to rid it of caked earth. Lezua and I helped to lift the large basin of cassavas onto mama's head. She had made a carriage gear out of used clothes, to enable her carry the basin without pains. Lezua had his tied in a sack-bag. I preferred the wheelbarrow. It was easier. And while I wheeled, I could stop, catch a grasshopper and then continue the journey. Under the bag or basin, I would drool and be constrained to multitask. It would be silly to stand under the weight of countless tubers of cassava just to catch a colourful grasshopper that required patience and special tactics. If mama caught me, that would be a different tale. I would get an awakening knock, such that could send for headache with speed.

It had drizzled before we set forth to the farm. Mama liked the light rain. It helped soften the soil, she said. Lezua and I whispered plans of revisiting the farm to set traps for rabbits, only if we could be sure of our way if we were to come alone. Mama didn't hear us. She was forbidden to hear our gossip. We spoke in such low tone that no one but us could grasp the discussion. If Mama heard us, all our activities would be monitored. Not because we would cause any serious damage to the crops on her farm but the days were evil. One woman from a distant compound had come to the house one evening with a story of how a certain woman in a nearby village had gone to the farm alone, without anyone to watch the environment for her, when some wannabe-rich-quick young man covered her head with a cement bag. When she could not breathe anymore, the man detached her head from her body and pocketed the head, leaving the body on her farm. When asked who saw the incident, the narrator hesitated and said a man who was hunting palm nuts had seen the incident all from his secured position. And when asked why the man didn't intervene to save the poor woman, he shrugged and said "world people!"

Lezua and I were to pack firewood to the fireplace where breakfast was made, and set fire after sweeping away the ash from the previous day's cooking. I was to put water in the kettle while he would do the sweeping. He had accepted the job half-heartedly. I lifted my end of the log of wood. Lezua who had not forgiven the wakeup incident attempted to lift his end but left the weight on my right leg. The sharp pain didn't permit an outright shout of hurt, it provoked revenge and I rushed at him swiftly with whatever I could find. When he dodged my first strike, which was nothing but air, he responded with an elder brother kind of knock. The heaviness of the knock released the tears that the log had prompted. I screamed. His narration was against me when Mama arrived at the scene. He apologised when they looked at him, but showed me his tongue when no one looked.

I lay on Mama's laps for the rest of the morning, sobbing from the pains. And by nightfall, my temperature had tripled. Lezua was apprehensive. He came by the mat where I was later transferred and apologised, sincerely, rubbing my head. He slept by my side for the night.

By morning, Mama was alarmed. My face had decorations of tiny balls of water, plastered there. She knew what it was but didn't like it. There was no money to buy calamine lotion. Whatever would pay for my medicine was in that cassava that had been tied and kept outside to dry so it would be sieved and fried. Mama stood over me and examined me with her eyes. Lezua could touch me. He had had his fair share of chicken pox before me. He was the one who went to Ekeere, the young chemist to get a bottle of the lotion. She would be paid later, Mama almost murmured.

The day went by lazily. Lezua sat by me. We watched neighbours who left for the farm in the morning return tired, with vegetables on their trays. We watched younger children who rode tyres retire under a shade to find some rest. And the shade shifted position, announcing the time of the day. It became darker and the sound of mortar and pestle began exchanged greetings. To someone who hadn't known of my health, I was a ghost. Lezua drowned me in the lotion.

I lay on the mat listening to the quiet and then its replacement. Frogs that had rented ponds created by rainfall of previous days began chorusing. Unlike some days when it meant noise, this day, it was music. The melody was only usual with calm listening. A frog with a deep voice would raise a song or conversation. Another would pick it up and so it continued. On nights when I wasn't on a mat, bathed in Calamine Lotion, Lezua and I would pick stones and target the voices. We only succeeded in securing silence for a while. When it was calm again, the chorus began. But no one stopped the sound this night and I loved it.

Through the competitive sound of mortars and pestles I heard legs shuffling. It was Waadu, the one who shared stories. Unplanned, Lezua adjusted from his spot on the mat to a less obvious part where he hid himself. Waadu walked in as noisily as she could be but her energetic steps dropped gradually when she noticed a boy, painted in white on a mat. I wriggled and she ran away, screaming of a ghost.

From a distance, people rushed to her for explanation and she pointed at our house. Mama appeared with a lantern, passing Lezua and I on the mat to the woman who was still being consoled. She asked what it was that had happened and was told of a ghost child. When neighbours gathered and walked into our house with all cautions, to see where the ghost lay, they found me and laughed heartily, concluding that Waadu's relationship with kai-kai was having an effect on her. But looking at me, on the mat, she shrugged and said "World people!"

NOTHINGNESS

NOTHINGNESS

The short walk to the piece of land where a grave had been dug for Kue was slow and tortuous. For Tambari, the hummed hymn from the church and intermittent wailing from someone were soundtracks to a lone journey, to the nothingness that had commenced. Her wish was for the black robe she wore to envelop her shame and allow her some living devoid of blames. Each footstep she took forward was a challenge. She had cried. Her eyes were covered. No. They were swollen and so was her thought, polarised.

And her tears, they were not really for Kue. They were hers. She was the bad one, the one who could not return early from the market to juggle washing the child and satisfying her man. When he came in, soaked in filth from the construction site, it was her fault to perceive his smell, to politely ask that he visit the bathroom first and then lie with her next. It was her fault that when he got angry she did persisted in not apologising for the something she couldn't place a finger on. Maybe if she did, just maybe he would have lived a day longer.

Kue, the one in the casket did not start out bad. No. He was not bad. He was just a tool in the hands of the gods—maybe. If he wasn't, he would have known that if any sane man placed Happiness Kuate and Tambari Saturday side by side, even the blind would choose Tambari. She was everything made with care and precision. The creator after filling her teeth parted the incisors. Just to show that he was the all-knowing creator, he touched her chins and made dimples out of them. When she smiled it was bliss, but that smile did not last so long. It grew older even by the time she was 24.

It had not always been about the fight. In short, Kue was all things perfect. He worked in the local church part time and at the construction site in town twice a week. He could read the bible fluently in English and in the local language. He had travelled to Port Harcourt, the Garden City. And Kue was hoping on one of the board chairmen of the harvest committees in the church, the one who grew up in Lagos, to introduce him into his trade of buying and selling used clothes. He never started out bad.

The first black-eye came from a punch one morning. She had allowed the water boil too much and the pap grew seeds. The bump on Tambari's forehead was not some extra wisdom begging to be set free. A travelling stool sent in flight caused it. Tambari had put his shoes in the ceiling to keep him from going out. She wanted him to spend his free day at home, with his family. When he asked for the shoes, it was her fault not to say that some demon had visited the house, looked around for anything, and decided on the new pair of shoes. After minutes of silence about the whereabouts of the shoes, she pointed to the ceiling and things flew.

The priest prayed that Kue may be received by the Lord he served until the evil one took over his mind. He had preached a day to his death about holiness and steadfastness in the faith. If Kue held on a little longer, maybe he would have been in the church premises sweeping and not lying lifeless on the wife of Piori. But Kue had everything but comportment when it involved a woman.

Tambari clutched a handful of sand and jerked in tears before letting it slide grain by grain into the grave of the man who could have lived, a man who she had fallen in love with when she first visited the village after 5 years in Port Harcourt as a house-help. He had met her on her way back from an errand for her mother and had asked about her name and father. When she refused, because he was too pushy and unrelenting, he told her that he had not come to play with her like other boys who licked the walls of a soup plate but left the plate once they tasted that which they wanted. He wanted to purchase the plate and not own it like a slave master. Nothing was sweeter than his words and she could remember what it was, her hand was in the hand of Kue who knelt and kissed it, like one of the things she watched on television. And maybe if she had resisted the urge to feel older at 23 because she had a bigger body, if she had insisted that he looked elsewhere, she wouldn't have become the widow of a man who died tragically between the thighs of the wife of a fellow church member.

THE SMALLNESS OF EVERYTHING

THE SMALLNESS OF EVERYTHING

A mobile phone which lay next to Ifechukwu livened. Its vibration was mild and non-distracting. Any other person wouldn't have noticed. But it was his phone. It was wired to his senses and the subconscious so even when his network sent a message for product advert he knew what it was without looking at the screen.

If it was put in silence mode and a call came through, he would feel it. He would look for the phone wherever it had been thrown and take the call before it rang no reply. But there have been tinier times when he could hear the ringing in his head and wouldn't see any correspondence in the phone. But when a message entered, without a beep, he knew it was a message and he responded.

The screen brightened like the face of a child whose mother has handed a piece of roasted yam, decorated with drops of palm oil and some sprinkled salt for taste. On his bed, he turned and picked up the device. He swiped it and smiled at the messages.

If the messages had come exactly forty-five minutes earlier he wouldn't have had the time to check at it. He couldn't have checked at anything for any reason. A man whose waist was in use cared little about the world around him and whatever cricket that whined.

"I am reading the book you sent me. It's so beautiful. I couldn't stop crying at the end of it. I feel I am related to the character."

She typed the sentences in a restless breath. And when he replied, it was with a smiley and then a word sentence and two words followed. "Cool. Have fun."

He was glad she liked the book. He bought books for friends. But when it was a lover, he was fond of buying them anything written by Chimamanda.

He didn't have a reason that may be too concrete to convince himself of the choice of the author. But maybe he did it because Ms Adichie didn't write so much of what is oblivious. She took the small realities that they were used to as young people in Nigeria and placed it in a book with flowery and sexy language. This, she has done in the four titles that had her name. And in this one, Ifemelu was the one who had represented Zikorah.

"I miss you."

He hesitated before he could reply. He missed her too. But when you dated someone who was overseas, someone who you were not ready to marry yet, you just become a bit careful about heaping emotions in everything. He was used to saying this. And even when he didn't think about it, it jumped into his mind.

"I miss you, Ife."

Ife knew that if he didn't say a thing to acknowledge the love that was in the air it was going to go stale and maybe at some point be left alone and rotten. And so in his fashion, he wrote her a poem, declaring his love, something she knew too well although she couldn't guess the words that would come each time.

Ife read anything every day. He read religious books and other forms of literature. Whatever he read became part of him. And the words stuck with him.

In this message he reminded her that though the distance was much it was good, that if she were closer, maybe there would have been a reason to get angry and stay away from each other since people who saw each other too often either took themselves for granted or became mundane.

They chatted until he was sleepy. And even when the message kept coming, his eyelids fell silently to the greater hand of sleep which was not pitiable. Or maybe it was not sleep. Maybe it was the other hand, of painted nails, of the one whose smiles could be touched, the one who lay next to him.

MANGO

MANGO

I held the two mangoes up as if I could tell how they were plucked, did they fall with the assistance of the wind or did someone who was too impatient climb the tree? Mother had put four mangoes on the garri she gave me when I was about to leave the village. She would have given more if I were to leave the next day but office work called. And Mother would not risk giving food to anyone from the village. Mother, though old, was careful about who held a thing she would eat or something she wanted to pass on to her children. She feared that someone could cast a spell of bad luck on it and I would be in ruin. It happens every day, she would say.

I called Chika to bring some water. It took her a while. She brought a bowl and I dropped the mangoes inside. She asked if she should wash them. I nodded. And as I lifted one of the mangoes, the memory flooded to my head. It was that same memory that had made me lift up the unwashed mangoes and given them a mad stare. I was very young, maybe ten. It was a quiet day in the village. Everyone had gone to the farm. I would not go. I disliked the farm like bitter leaf soup. I disliked work on the farm. If I was going there to hunt grasshoppers, I wouldn't mind but they would not even let me have a tiny moment for myself.

I roamed the village until the spirit which led me brought me under a mango tree in my mother's compound. I sat there and looked up the tall tree. It was really tall and I dwarfed at its base. The wind passed. I prayed that it should bring down some mangoes. It did not throw down any. I sat and nothing heard my voice. Maybe I was dizzy when I heard a sound not too far from where I sat. It would be a mango; I said to myself and went in search of it. Luckily, after lifting a couple of rotten leafs I saw it, ripped, a bit robust and innocently waiting for me. I picked it up like a jewel, something I had waited for.

I sat down, cleaned the mango on my cloth and ate the first layer. It sank into me and I must have closed my eyes when Lenu, the tomboy walked in. She watched me eat with envy. I did not say a word. She looked up the tree, as if praying for the entire tree to fall so she could take mangoes to her home and never lack again. I ate and licked on the seed and almost swallowed it when an unusual wind blew. Such wind came with surprises, so I dropped the seed and got ready for anything. Lenu did not look at me again. She kept her attention on the tree and I could see that she was wishing something bigger than I could understand.

The wind came and went. Nothing happened. I sat back and kept a glance at her, her fair body and stony face. She could beat up a boy and anyone who made to help. I had never fought with her and would not. She did not play in the sand like other children. She cooked or rode tyres. She went to the evening market, gathered her soup items and discarded tomato containers and cooked in them.

A mango dropped. Swiftly, Lenu ran after it. I did too. She dived at the spot where it fell. I dived at the spot too. We struggled. She was closer to it than I was. We struggled some more but she reached it and turned around. I was on her, already with a choice of snatching the mango away or allowing fate to bring me another one. But what if the one I ate was my last? I looked at her and saw beamed smiles.

Lenu did not eat hers. She held on to it like it was an akara. I looked at her when I could and devised a means to getting the mango. Another small wind blew. Two mangoes fell. Before I could get up Lenu had the first and was looking for the second. I dived at the spot and held it down. And she stood over me, as if to beat me up, but she dropped her mango and kissed me.

*****

Chika called from the room for a mango. I quickly shook water off one and took it to her but the memory of the incident could not leave me. Did I beg her to do what she did or was I forced to do it? The baby woke up and I rushed to carry her. Chika ate on her mango without a knife. I looked upon her with some admiration. She smiled back, unaware of the memory every bite on the mango brought.

A TINY PLACE CALLED HAPPINESS

A TINY PLACE CALLED HAPPINESS

I was the one who was yanked off a sleeping mat and pulled behind Ika, even though grandmother says a child has to be fully awakened before he is carried from his place of sleep so his spirit does not leave him. I was the one who missed steps and fell and rose again. And spurred to cry but held on to Ika's wrapper until she held my wrist firmly and pulled me through uneven paths walled by thick grasses that were taller than me. I was the one who ran to keep pace with her and not cry, because she must not have two people crying while she was looking for safety.

I was the one without a shirt or pants or slippers, the one elephant grasses brushed against his body and rubbed against his thing, the one used for peeing, because my other hand held life, wrapped in a cellophane bag.

Kara was the one who was strapped to Ika's back, the one who cried, and when her voice dropped it was not because she stopped crying but her thumb was stuck inside her small mouth. Kara was the one who came months ago, in the midwife's house, the one who made papa to stop visiting. When papa saw her pink face it was not his, mother's, grandmother's, or grandfather's. Kara was the one with a strange luck— the one born in a time when our people and the people across the rivers waged a war.

I was the one who, when we stopped at the forest where mother said was safe, asked if we could chew on the garri and the salt that she had wrapped in the cellophane bag. And I was the one mother looked at with bloodshot eyes, like I was the enemy from the other side of the rivers, the ones who had sent us packing from the house. I was the one who dropped the bag and pushed it to her side and looked around to avoid her eyes. I was the one whose tears dropped on his belly and when mother discovered it, she knocked my head and the held cry picked up and rang through our safe zone. Kara was the one mother rocked so she would not cry like me.

It was the enemy that fired the guns that woke mother and the rest of the villagers. It was the enemy that made one family dig a trench few meters from their house and hide inside. Their house was beautiful and it had many treasured things. They could not leave it totally. The man of the house swore to see the face of the ringleader of the enemies who would be the first to fire a shot at his padlock and go inside to carry his steel trunk on his head and order his soldiers to do same and look around for a living soul so they could shoot at the terrified one and laugh and go home.

It was mother, in her uncertainty of our safety when the sounds of guns drew nearer, that held my hand and forced me to close my eyes and pray that we should not be seen and that our heads should be saved so that all glory would return to God. But I was the one who did not close my eyes, the one who looked at a scarecrow in a distance and wondered if it was God, for its wide open hands were stoic and unflinching despite the many sounds of guns and the cries. I was the one who wished we could find happiness again, like the days when I would not have to be yanked off the mat but would be tapped and taken to the backyard to ease myself. And mother would bring out a bucket of water and ask me to hold its rim while she scrubbed my leg.

THE ONE WHO WAS GIFTED WITH THE MIND OF A CHILD

THE ONE WHO WAS GIFTED WITH THE MIND OF A CHILD

Beside the dull, gazing eyes which sat in their hollow boxes, penetrating and soul-hunting yet childlike, the other thing uncle Legbo returned with, besides a skeletal structure; a shadow of a once well-built pride of his community, was an old brown leather box, stripped of its essence, the colour wearing away into emptiness. Devoid of clothes and filled with papers that were scribbled with the name of the demon that pushed him left, right and centre, the box was a symbol of what life held for him, nothing.

Each letter of the name of the demon stood apart, as if scared of closeness. It spelt JESSICA and a note followed: "a piggy idiotic ingrate, full of nothingness but cursed oxygen. When you snore, the world collapses and sleep is postponed, and everything is reversed, even goodness, fresh air, and sanity." The note did not say whether Jessica was the one he cheated on, the one who took his name to a medicine man who exchanged it for that of a child.

Until uncle Legbo's hands and legs were tied and brought back to the village, Kaanayiga, the boy who lived with him in the city said uncle became a second means of entertainment on his street in Lagos. Whenever outdoor preachers did not bring actors to stage being sick and receiving healing, uncle Legbo danced for the crowd at no fee. He danced even when the speakers did not play music. He danced when someone spoke in tongues and called the names of the streets in Lagos or the names of God in a local language.

Kaanayiga said his apartment was given out to another tenant who was carefree about the previous occupant whose appliances were still in there. The tenant allowed him to sleep outside the apartment for a week until he chased him away. He said whenever uncle Legbo approached the door for anything, maybe a peep at the random images on his own TV set, the new occupant picked up a large stick and chased after him to the end of the world, where curses, untrimmed, poured on him.

When all forms of healing failed, the only thing Papa and Kaanayiga could do was to bring him home. But that too was uneasy. He had to be followed calmly and drugged. It was in his drugged state that he was tied and brought to Dukana.

Uncle stared at anyone who looked at him. He wouldn't blink. He would not say a word. He sat on a wooden stool that Papa made for him. It was there that his meals were served, day and night. It was there that he slept. And on cold nights, he crawled to any opened veranda.

Sometimes, on his stool, he looked like a baby king, innocent but ragged. Sometimes he appeared with so much dignity and clear cut poise such that royalties possessed but for his dull eyes. He never sagged his head in despair. Anyone who looked at him knew that he was not a happy man. He might have lost his mind but he did not lose the thing that burdened him. He held it up so much that someone who was a visitor, someone who had visited Dukana for the first time would bow to him in greetings and enquire politely where a road led or what the name of whoever they were looking for was.

Maybe uncle was a king, for no one disturbed him. He was not sent on any errand; asked to break firewood or made to peel the cassava we had uprooted from a hard earth. The worst he got was a carefree plea by Mother to help her watch over the house and the yam barn especially. And like someone who was absent, whose mind was elsewhere, he let the words pour on him without effect.

Uncle's demons beat a fierce drum one weekend. A certain chubby lady who had stayed in Lagos, who the village birds, including Kaanayiga whispered that she stayed in his place when the good days were still good, walked into the compound. Uncle's eyes stayed on her until she sat beside him and sobbed. She asked if this was truly Legbo, a man who walked the streets of Orile and women who were in the arms of their husbands quivered and winked and called out to him. She looked at him with eyes welled up in tears. The lady dropped her handbag and walked across the yard. She approached a kiosk and returned with a pair of scissors. With it, she trimmed his beards and wiped his face with handkerchief she pulled out of her handbag. And uncle Legbo, like one liberated of a curse, turned around and looked at the lady with a smile, for the first time since he came home. He took her hand mildly, rubbed it carefully and dropped it. Papa who watched from his doorpost gasped at the drama. Uncle Legbo took the scissors from the lady, flipped it gently and slit his own wrist. And the lady, shocked and overwhelmed by uncle's action, cried and shook him but it was life that was gushing out of him in form of blood.

THE PREACHER

THE PREACHER

You know how the prayer starts. She pleads with everyone to simply appreciate the creator of mankind for his lavished grace upon earth. It is polite. Who won't permit such a humble offer? Then you would think that in thirty seconds the prayer would be summarized. And you wait, but it lingers like palm oil dripping down the mouth of a child struggling to feed himself. And you become glad a little, that at least you would resume listening to some music in the next second. But you are wrong, dead wrong.

You had put a track on pause when the full framed lady, with hair wrapped in a piece of cloth that seemed like it had never seen water and soap, greeted passengers in the name of Jesus. Your headphone hung around your neck, hoping that what she was going to say would be as brief as possible, for your earlobes, itchy, awaited the headphone, a place it had been for less than an hour. You had bought it because of the young woman who sat in front of the shop. It was her elevated chest and the warmness of her eyes each time she beckoned at a customer that drove you to her, but then that's unnecessary information.

And you had also spent a lot of time queuing for the bus ticket and wishing all things would just disappear so you would be on your way home, to the arm of your bed; a more sincere friend, one that won't ever lie to you or say you had spent much time in its bosom. And the beggars who sang kept a rhythm of a bad song in your head and cleared up all thoughts of failed relationship. At least their call to Bari to reward you with twin babies was amusing enough. You had no girlfriend. How could you even have babies? In short, the one whom you called a girlfriend left before the New Year. A phone conversation had made everything blank. You had wondered how a tiny conversation with little shouting could end the passion you guys shared. But then, that's history.

The preacher, led by spirits that would not treat her with kindness, for they stuck with her and dragged her onto more prayer points, called on all the familiar angels you had read in the bible. You had not read anything anywhere. You had heard the names by accident. You were always there, in the Sunday school classes, folding tiny papers and throwing them at those who had their concentration on God. And one day, the teacher had told you of Gabriel, the archangel who would come down and do to your backside what world people did to the skin of Jesus in that Mel Gibson's movie. That was how you knew the name. It was an unforgettable memory.

You open your eyes. You look around to see if there was anyone who is equally bored of the prayer. You see no eyes. The people around you had their eyes closed tightly in reverence. You resume the eyes closing and keep wishing the prayer would end. It stops. And she calls on those who want to give their lives to Christ. You are born again, you reassure yourself. At least you are free of this one. The request for the blackened sinner is insistent. You open your eyes a little and see the eyes of the preacher on you. You close it quickly. The voice seems to face you. The saliva sprinkles all over your face. You try to lick your lips but you taste something foul. You curse in your spirit but a voice is over your head. It is becoming more specific. The driver is not stopping anywhere. You scream: "I want piss, driver." And the man ignores it. You bang on the roof. All eyes are open and staring at you. You are angry and the driver listens and finally brings the bus to a stop. You alight in fury, unzipping your trousers for the urine which you wish would end all things which troubled your soul. But there is murmuring back in the bus. Maybe the bus people were angry too and would use cello tape on her mouth. Or she has called you the chosen one who was handpicked by Satan himself to destroy the precious lives on the bus by an accident or anything else. The eyes in the bus stare at you, suspecting, and yours wouldn't leave theirs. When you settle down and place your headphone over your ears, giant hands quickly grip you down. There is the sprinkling of holy water and holy spits and chants of Holy Ghost fire on you. You must be saved.

STARS

STARS

Papa came home one day and walked across the television set. He pinned a piece of wrapper on the wall. When he walked away from it, I saw a six-star dotted blue, yellow and green flag. "It is a symbol of what would come; our eventual freedom from Nigeria," he said. "Soon, we will be carved out of the mistake called Nigeria and the oil pipelines which lie across our farmlands in Wiibara would cease to produce money for the government." He said when the time comes, I too, like those I read of, who were sent to Eton, would pack my bag and join the special breed of boys who were being groomed to rule over the universe.

Papa saluted the flag, like a soldier, one whose salutation was not obligatory as ordered by an authority but one whose drive was internal, unseen but intense. He withdrew his snuff box from his trousers' pocket still staring at the small flag or Biaka, his girlfriend. He tapped its cover twice—a ritual I had witnessed unnumbered times. He opened it and his eyes left the flag for the snuff. Papa's eyes glistened at the sight of the brownness or the consolation of it being available or its significance, that someday, one day, there would be so much snuff in the box, so much that he would share and still have more to sniff.

With the tip of his index finger, he raised a lump into one of his nostrils and inhaled heavily. His breath stopped. His eyes welled with water. When he could breathe again, he repeated the same act to his other nostril and let out series of sneezes. I stood up from the wooden stool he had made for me and brought him water in a small basin. It was a tradition, to bring him water when he was downing his snuff. Sometimes the sneeze is the cue. Other times, a tiny voice whispers to me.

Bringing him water was something I could do with my eyes closed. I didn't negotiate the amount of water in the basin each time of need. They didn't grow fuller with the years. It was just a cup, just one and nothing more. If you added some jara, playfully, Papa would ask for an empty bucket and would empty a part in the bucket, precisely the amount that was graciously added. We didn't lack water in the village. Papa just liked his things moderate.

While Papa sniffed, he told me how he has joined the men and women who were to bring the Ogoni kingdom to us in the village. He said he registered with MOSOP and those who were not members may not benefit from the kingdom's goodness. He asked how school was and requested to see what it was that we did in school. He brushed his tobacco-stained hand and the mucus-glued finger on his trousers and flipped through the workbook I handed to him. When he got to the page where I was to fill in the blank space, he asked for a pencil and held my hand to fill it.

"If the oil companies that would come to our new kingdom pay compensation money for the spoiled farmland and polluted water, I will get you new clothes and send you to Eton." He meant it. He meant whatever he said when he didn't look at me.

***

And so the flag became part of us. We slept in its presence and woke with its promise. It stared at me and I stared at it. I asked why it had six stars, whether the stars on it were representative of the uncounted stars we saw in the sky at night and Papa smiled and rubbed my head gently. He told me that stars were special, that they represented distant lights that lead, that when a people walked towards it and followed their hearts, like the wise men in the bible, their destinations were usually coloured and divinely reached. He said the future for us in Dukana was not different from what we read in the bible.

If a fly perched on the flag, Papa didn't treat it cruelly. He didn't like it either. He carefully chased it and went hard on it when it fled the flag.

In the village, Papa became teeh, a sign of respect. He had joined a special group that was charged with questioning the oil people and the government about our prolonged kingdom. Anyone Papa met, he told about the future, the brightness and the need to be hopeful, to write things that they would do with money when it arrived. He told them that no man's mind functioned when the money arrived, that all the mind cared about was spending. He held me by the hand. And when more questions than expected poured from the mouths of the eager villagers I felt his palm become sweaty.

I accompanied Papa on his house-to-house visits. I was with him when he told Biaka, Pastor Leyere-ue's unmarried daughter that his own tomorrow was now assured and that maybe, if he completes his diploma programme at the Polytechnic in Bori, he would be considered for the post of the president of MOSOP. I was there when Biaka's heart leapt and caused her to melt in love right there in our presence, in the sun that had stayed hot all day. It was the melted heart which caused Biaka to moan on those many nights they thought I was asleep, those nights I was given a wrapper to spread on the floor because someone who was special would visit. It was one of those nights, in the presence of the naughtiness that I stared at the stars in the flag and saw Eton, its glory and my presence interlocked.

A DAY GONE WRONG

A DAY GONE WRONG

One Saturday evening when the sun had retired from its place in the sky and large lazy darkness was creeping in on earth's people; the poor jostling from wherever a benevolent spirit had led them and the rich, putting finishing touches on the clothes to be worn to church the next day, Jesus, in his wondrous ways, pushed uncle Nuka to the small field at the end of the street where Legbo and I were busy. We were strategising on what to do with the next day's offering; to buy some chin-chin in school the day after Sunday or go to the game house few minutes after school hour with whatever we would get.

Uncle Nuka, whose whereabouts we did not know of for a week, appeared like a ghost from a cheap sitcom. First, we doubted the image we saw. Very unclearly in a distance, we saw a man who almost leaped, for his walk was not that of Nuka who would not leap for anything, except if it was some requirements by Lesi. But as he approached, and we could see from where an afro hair style began, we could not doubt it any longer that though lost for a week or so, uncle Nuka was back to the community. Suanu and I rose to greet him. He waved us down and stared into whatever space it was that endeared him.

When whatever he was communicating with gave him some space, uncle Nuka sent us, as usual, to go two streets away to call him his girlfriend, Lesi, against our protest that the road that led to Lesi's house was bad. One needed to be an athlete to jump over the pool of water and then navigate around the several strategically positioned excreta by the dozens of idiotic children who lived in the estate. And even if we could go, we had been hungry all day and there would be no more strength left in us, after the long walk, to enable the navigation to Lesi's.

Maybe uncle Nuka was a seer or something like that because he looked at Legbo and me intently for maybe ten seconds and placed a crisp two hundred naira note in my hand without saying anything. Confused whether the sum was for the one whom he sought to see or for those whose discomfort must be endured for one man to satisfy his many desires, we looked at him and then the money until he gestured that the money was for us, our price for being vain. And we didn't wait for further persuasion. We had all we needed to climb Everest.

When we saw the hurdles that made Lesi's house phenomenal, we jumped, and when it got to the part where we had to hold our nose up and kill all sense of smell, we did it with ease. And each time the courage to hold on threatened to fail, we looked at the two hundred naira note and regained enormous courage. We made it into the compound and proceeded to climb the grease stained staircase without handrails. Maybe the landlord had forgotten to add handrails or he knew that the kind of tenants he would get would not mind, for no one who lived in Man-Must-Whack Estate complained that a child could fall or that an old woman needed assistance.

Legbo went ahead while I followed. We knew the drill. We were just passing by to greet auntie Lesi, if we were accosted by her father or mother. If we met her siblings, we could as well say: Lesiwa, uncle Nuka wants to sleep with you, he has sent us to inform you so, for her siblings were independent. The youngest child who was still in primary school, comfortable in same class for four years, had four older boyfriends on our street and uncountable ones miles away from our street. Robbed of height but not energy to stand by the road at ten in the night, to caress a man who could be close to her father's age, Lesi's sister, Aanu was a strong breed.

Aanu was probably cursed from when she was a baby. We had heard that one time when they had gone to the village for Christmas, Aanu who was not supposed to follow her siblings to the stream had done so without approval and when she met a sacrificial bar of soap at the foot of the water, she quickly un-wrapped it and bathed with it. Her size and gift of meeting men were consolations from the gods who remained unwashed because of her silliness.

At the door, Legbo knocked. There was no response. Usually, the sound of a television, of an actor on TV screaming a proverb in wrong English, in an address to a god, would have been heard. And if the door was answered and her parents saw us, they would ask us in and ask if our parents knew we had wandered that way. But the stillness of the room provoked more knocks and soon Legbo and I found a new play tool.

Maybe it was hammer or something weightier that was used because two minutes after, we could still hear voices but couldn't tell where we were after two distinguished knocks landed on our heads. It was Mueka, Lesi's elder brother, the one we all knew as a thief but wouldn't dare to insinuate it even in our dreams, the one whose favourite pastime was to bully and send one on an errand with less money for an item. He kept laughing while we died under the pains of the knock.

Maybe we were carried down stairs or pushed to the pool of mud water, and particles of things we strongly felt were connected to the heaps by the dozens of children bathed us. While we cried and mourned a day gone wrong, a confirmation that I still had the two hundred naira note in my pocket, though soaked, meant everything beautiful.

Acknowledgements

The first feeling of fulfilment that enwrapped me when I first visited Nsukka in 2012 must have been what sustained me throughout my four years stay. I felt at rest to be in an environment that had seen some very distinguished Nigerian writers.

I have to appreciate Writivism for the story "In the Dark". I worked on it after the creative writing workshop in Abuja, Nigeria in 2014. "Slum Diary" won Second Place at the Creative Wings Short Story contest organised by Ugreen Foundation in 2011. "How to say Goodbye" was published in the Ake Review of 2015, for the Ake Arts Festival. "Like Eyes Liquid with Hope" won First Place at the Literary Week of the Department of English and Literary Studies, University of Nigeria, Nsukka in 2015. "Port Harcourt" was published on Brittle Paper. I appreciate the show of love.

Thank you, Lucky and Lesiwa Nwilo; my parents – I'd choose you two again in my next life. Oluchi Nchege, you made Nsukka home, with care and love. Leyii Kwanee gave me a lift to tertiary education. Uloma Onyebuchi is a mother. Ledum Mitee listens when it is noisy out there. Timi-Nipre has a heart of gold. Joe Aito, thanks for reading the manuscript. Naomi Lucas is friend. Nyiedum Ufot is a sister. Barilee Inania is a former classmate turned sister. Mary Lenu Nkasi, Affion Ene-Obong, Binyerem Ukonu, Toni Kan, Eedee Goneh, Dorka John-Ziah, Grace Ewonubari, Raymond Webilor Jnr., Mrs. Damka Ideye, Ndume Green, Rev. Sister Jane-Patrick Okolie, Chidinma Chukwuonye are dear to my heart. Prince Smart is brother and designer. Ebenezer Agu and Johnson Urama Jnr. are helpful copy-editors, Chioma Chukwunedu is friend. Prof. Damian Opata, Fidelis Okoro and Rev. Paul Igbara you guys are miracle workers. I appreciate Dr Owens Wiwa for everything—care and funds—when I almost dropped out of school. Femi Morgan is enviably energetic. And to others who can't be listed, thank you, always.

Author

BURA-BARI NWILO was born in Port Harcourt in Rivers State in September 1987. His description of life in primary and secondary schools is 'darkly fond'. Bura-Bari studied English and Literature at the University of Nigeria, Nsukka.

His stories and poems have appeared in Saraba Magazine, Sentinel Nigeria, Brittle Paper, the ANA Review, Ake Review, Bookslive.co.za, GuerillaBasement, Muwado, Guardian Nigeria, the defunct 234Next newspaper, Muse Journal of the Department of English and Literary Studies, University of Nigeria, Nsukka and the Nwokike Arts Journal.

His 'rotten' English short story, Like Eyes Liquid with Hope was long-listed for the 2016 Writivism short story prize. It will be published in French and English in 2016. Nwilo participated at the 2013 creative writing workshop organised by the Wole Soyinka Foundation in Lagos, Nigeria. Nwilo is also the 2016 winner of WAW 100 Words flash fiction contest.

Printed in the United States
by Baker & Taylor Publisher Services